THE NEED TO KNOW LIBRARY™

EVERYTHING YOU NEED TO KNOW ABOUT SMOKING, VAPING, AND YOUR HEALTH

SHERRI MABRY GORDON

Rosen YA
New York

Published in 2019 by The Rosen Publishing Group, Inc.
29 East 21st Street, New York, NY 10010

Copyright © 2019 by The Rosen Publishing Group, Inc.

First Edition

All rights reserved. No part of this book may be reproduced in any form without permission in writing from the publisher, except by a reviewer.

Library of Congress Cataloging-in-Publication Data

Names: Gordon, Sherri Mabry, author.
Title: Everything you need to know about smoking, vaping, and your health /
Sherri Mabry Gordon.
Description: First edition. | New York : Rosen Young Adult, 2019. | Series: The need to know library | Audience: Grades 7–12. | Includes bibliographical references and index.
Identifiers: LCCN 2018006564| ISBN 9781508183525 (library bound) | ISBN 9781508183518 (paperback)
Subjects: LCSH: Smoking—Health aspects—Juvenile literature. | Youth—Tobacco use—Juvenile literature.
Classification: LCC HV5745 .G58 2019 | DDC 613.85—dc23
LC record available at https://lccn.loc.gov/2018006564

Manufactured in the United States of America

CONTENTS

INTRODUCTION..4

CHAPTER ONE
WHAT ARE PEOPLE SMOKING ANYWAY?..............................7

CHAPTER TWO
UNDERSTANDING ADDICTION...16

CHAPTER THREE
HEALTH IMPACTS OF SMOKING AND VAPING.....................26

CHAPTER FOUR
BE A QUITTER!...36

CHAPTER FIVE
CHOOSING TO BE SMOKE FREE...45

GLOSSARY...54
FOR MORE INFORMATION..56
FOR FURTHER READING...59
BIBLIOGRAPHY..60
INDEX...62

INTRODUCTION

Amanda tried her first cigarette when she was just eleven years old. In her mind, there was nothing wrong with what she was doing, never mind the fact that she was only in fifth grade. By the time she was thirteen, she was smoking every day. Whether she stole cigarettes from her parents or bought a pack on her way home from school, she found a way to smoke.

To her, it was normal. After all, her parents, friends, and the older kids that she looked up to all smoked. "I thought I should smoke too," she says. Smoking helped her feel like she fit in. By the time Amanda reached high school, she was skipping classes to smoke. It was then that she realized she had a problem. That problem was called addiction.

But Amanda didn't feel motivated to quit. Not even watching her grandfather, also a smoker, die of lung cancer was enough to make her quit. It wasn't until her first child was born prematurely that she finally gave up smoking.

"I feel a tremendous amount of guilt for my daughter being born early," Amanda says. "I knew that smoking was bad [during pregnancy but] I didn't think it would happen to me. I didn't think I would have a premature baby. I didn't think my child would have asthma."

To quit smoking, Amanda focused on other ways to relieve stress rather than grabbing a cigarette. For example, she used prayer, exercise, and distraction

INTRODUCTION | 5

Smoking and vaping are harmful during pregnancy. Doing so can cause babies to be born prematurely and can lead to asthma and other issues later in life.

to handle her stress so that she wouldn't use smoking as a way to cope. "Smoking has a caused a lot of pain in my life. I lost my grandfather to lung cancer. I had my first child two months early. My dad, who I smoked many cigarettes with, now has stage four lung cancer, and I [hope] by sharing the pain and the hurt that smoking has caused in my life, that it will help people quit smoking."

Every day, nearly four thousand kids under the age of eighteen try their first cigarette, according to the Centers for Disease Control and Prevention

(CDC). That's almost 1.5 million teens a year. Meanwhile, e-cigarettes are growing in popularity. Twice as many teens vape as smoke, according to a 2017 report by the surgeon general. Many teens choose to vape instead of smoking because they believe vaping is safer than smoking. Safer is not the same as safe, though, and research shows that e-cigarettes are associated with numerous health risks.

The CDC reports that if young people do not start using tobacco by the age of twenty-six, they are unlikely to pick up the habit. By learning the facts about the health risks of smoking and vaping and how addiction really works, teens can better understand what it takes to quit smoking and vaping before it's too late, or, ideally, never start in the first place.

CHAPTER ONE

WHAT ARE PEOPLE SMOKING ANYWAY?

Most young people know that smoking and vaping are unhealthy habits, yet millions of teens continue to smoke and vape. In the United States alone, more than 3.6 million middle school and high school students smoke cigarettes, according to the CDC, and 99 percent of all smokers have started by the time they are twenty-six. Meanwhile, the CDC reports that more than three million kids in middle and high school vape every month.

For those who do start smoking or vaping, the outlook is not good. Many cigarette smokers develop diseases such as lung cancer, heart disease, and even a condition known as Buerger's disease, which reduces blood flow to the arms and legs. Most smokers become addicted and experience changes in behavior and appearance. According to the CDC, most cigarette smokers die thirteen years earlier than their peers who do not smoke.

Many teens choose vaping over smoking out of a belief that vaping is safer than smoking. While they are not as dangerous as traditional cigarettes, most e-cigarettes contain chemicals that can be extremely

The outlook for smokers is not good. Besides developing all sorts of diseases, smokers die an average of thirteen years earlier than their peers, according to the CDC.

harmful. Also, just like cigarettes, e-cigarettes contain nicotine, which makes them highly addictive.

A CLOSER LOOK AT WHAT TEENS ARE SMOKING

While the numbers of teens smoking traditional cigarettes has decreased, overall tobacco use by teens remains steady, according to WebMD. This is because teen use of e-cigarettes is on the rise. In addition to

VAPING IN CLASS?

A Juul is a brand of e-cigarette device that is increasingly popular among teenagers. Resembling a flash drive and small enough to fit into a closed fist, the Juul has become a source of concern for teachers and parents because of the way it allows teens to vape discreetly, even in class.

An anonymous fifteen-year-old quoted on Offspring described trying a Juul for the first time in the school lunchroom. "It hurt my throat more than anything else I've done. I hit it and coughed immediately. At first it was just fun and it was something that you could do anywhere. It's so easy. Then it just became something I was doing nonstop, but I still felt a buzz. Now, I go crazy if I don't have it."

A 2017 study in the journal *Pediatrics* suggests that discreet vaping devices such as the Juul may be introducing a new generation of teenagers to nicotine, leading to addiction and making them more likely to take up smoking traditional cigarettes later.

cigarettes and e-cigarettes, many teens also smoke marijuana or use smokeless tobacco, hookahs, or bidis.

TRADITIONAL CIGARETTES

Filled with tobacco and sold in packages at just about every corner market, gas station, and grocery store, cigarettes are the leading cause of preventable deaths in the

United States. In fact, they often cause cancer, heart disease, and lung disease, as well as a slew of other health issues. Traditional cigarettes consist of tobacco, chemical additives, a filter, and a paper wrapping. The smoke inhaled from a burning cigarette contains a mix of more than seven thousand harmful chemicals. What's more, there is no evidence that cigarettes that are advertised as organic, natural, or additive free are any safer than regular cigarettes.

E-CIGARETTES

E-cigarettes, also called vape pens, vapes, or e-cigs, are battery-operated devices used to deliver nicotine,

Many kids use e-cigarettes, also called vape pens, vapes, or e-cigs, because they feel they are safer than traditional cigarettes.

flavorings, and other additives to users via an inhaled aerosol. They also can be used as a delivery system for marijuana and other drugs. E-cigarettes heat a liquid into an aerosol that the user inhales. E-cigarettes are available in a wide variety of flavors including many that are appealing to teens. Yet, the chemicals they are inhaling are toxic. The ingredients can contain nicotine, ultrafine particles, a chemical known as diacetyl, which is linked to lung disease, benzene, which is found in car exhaust, and metals such as nickel, tin, and lead.

SMOKELESS TOBACCO

Commonly referred to as chew, dip, or spit tobacco, it can come in a variety of different forms. Sometimes it is finely-ground tobacco that is either dry or moist. When it is dry it is powder-like and is often inhaled. When it is moist, it is placed between the gums and cheek. Other times, the tobacco comes in strips, is shredded, or is shaped like a plug. The most common form is loose-leaf tobacco that has been sweetened and comes in a foil pouch or can. People who use smokeless tobacco may suffer gum loss, cancer, stained teeth, and mouth sores.

MARIJUANA

Usually when kids use marijuana or pot they are smoking joints. Typically, these joints contain dried marijuana material rolled with tobacco into a cigarette. Some users mix it into food, like brownies, or use it to brew tea. Sometimes other drugs like PCP or crack cocaine are added to the joint, increasing the risks significantly. According to a study by Monitoring the Future, one in five high school students surveyed admitted to using marijuana in the past month. Although the health risks of marijuana use are less severe than cigarette use, it can be addictive, and long-term marijuana use can lead to lung-related health problems. Marijuana is legal for adults over twenty-one years in some states and illegal in others.

HOOKAHS

Smoking a hookah, also known as a water pipe, is usually a social activity. Typically, people sit around a table and pass a hookah around. Inside the hookah, flavored tobacco is heated and filtered by water. This substance then passes through a hose to the mouthpiece where it is inhaled. Just like traditional cigarette use, hookah use can lead to cancer, heart disease, and lung disease. What's more, because multiple people use the same mouthpiece, there also is a risk of spreading other diseases like herpes, tuberculosis, and hepatitis.

BIDIS

Flavored with kid-friendly flavors like chocolate or cherry, bidis are hand-rolled, leaf-wrapped cigarettes tied with a

WHAT ARE PEOPLE SMOKING ANYWAY? | 13

Smoking a hookah, also known as a water pipe, is a social activity that is growing in popularity. Typically, flavored tobacco is heated and filtered by water.

string at both ends. Despite their childlike appeal, bidis come with the same risks as cigarettes, and in fact they contain three to five times more nicotine than cigarettes.

WHY TEENS SMOKE AND VAPE

According to the American Lung Association, most kids in elementary school believe they will never take up smoking. But as they get older, their opinions and influences change, and many become open to smoking. There are a vast number of reasons why teens and young adults

When teens see celebrities smoking, they may start to see smoking as hip and glamorous.

might begin smoking or vaping. These include everything from peer pressure and wanting to fit in to rebellion, curiosity, and social influences. Cigarette companies and even some celebrities portray smoking as cool, sexy, fun, attractive, and edgy, and kids see these images all around them. Many kids think of smoking as something that allows them to establish their independence from the adults in their lives who are telling them not to smoke. At the same time, teens are more likely to smoke if the adults in their lives smoke.

When teens start smoking, they usually feel like they have control over their habit and that they can quit at any time. Only 5 percent of high school smokers think they will still be smoking five years after they graduate, but the reality is that 75 percent of teen smokers will still be using some form of tobacco as adults, according to Smokefree.gov. The problem is, quitting is hard. And teens often do not realize that until it is too late.

MYTHS AND FACTS

MYTH: I can quit smoking at any time.

FACT: Young brains are highly susceptible to addiction, and when an addiction forms, the brain is rewired to crave the substance. As a result, it is not easy to quit smoking. While it is possible to quit, it is very hard, and most people make several attempts to quit smoking or vaping before they are successful. A 2011 study by the CDC showed that 70 percent of smokers wanted to quit, more than half had tried to quit in the previous year, and only 6 percent had succeeded.

MYTH: Vaping (or using e-cigarettes) is a safe alternative to traditional cigarettes.

FACT: Any time you inhale anything other than oxygen into your lungs, you run the risk of damage. Many e-cigarettes contain the chemical diacetyl, which has been linked to a respiratory disease called bronchiolitis obliterans. What's more, research shows that teens who use e-cigarettes are more likely to try other forms of smoking than those who have never vaped.

MYTH: Smoking makes me feel happy and energetic.

FACT: Initially, smoking may make you feel energized, especially because your body has never experienced nicotine before. But after continued use, as your body becomes more dependent on the substances you are inhaling, you will no longer feel that way. In fact, research has shown that teens who are exposed to nicotine are at a higher risk for mood disorders such as depression.

CHAPTER TWO

UNDERSTANDING ADDICTION

When he was eleven or twelve years old, Nick started smoking cigarettes. He continued to smoke for years, to the point where he lost his sense of taste and smell. Then, when he was eighteen, he switched to e-cigarettes because he thought they were safer. "It's the lesser of two evils," Nick says. But is that true?

Because e-cigarettes are newer than traditional cigarettes, there is less research out there about them, but based on the studies that have been done, there is cause for concern. In fact, e-cigarettes can be just as addictive as traditional cigarettes, and they have been linked to some serious health risks.

"Safer is not the same as safe," says Brian King, deputy director for research translation in the CDC's Office on Smoking and Health. "Nicotine is a prime ingredient in these devices. [And] studies show nicotine is more addictive than heroin or cocaine. [What's more,] there is a growing body of evidence that nicotine can harm the developing adolescent brain."

UNDERSTANDING ADDICTION | 17

Most teens don't expect to smoke all of their lives. But nicotine is a powerful chemical that rewires the brain. Once you start smoking or vaping, it's very hard to stop.

Yet, the number of teens using e-cigarettes has skyrocketed. "High school students are using e-cigarettes at a greater rate than adults," King says. And they can't seem to stop because they are addicted."

SMOKING, VAPING, AND YOUR BRAIN

When you are a teen, the part of your brain that is responsible for making decisions is not fully developed. For this reason, young people often take more risks

Three out of four teens who smoke in high school will still be smoking as adults, according to Smokefree.gov.

than people who are older. Because the teen brain is still developing and changing, teens who smoke or vape are at a greater risk of damaging their brains in the long term. Nicotine has a powerful impact on their developing brains. Aside from becoming addicted, teens who smoke and vape may also develop mood disorders, and their ability to control impulses may be permanently impacted. Even a person's attention span and learning abilities can be affected by nicotine. In fact, according to a University of California, Los Angeles study, the more addicted a teen is to nicotine, the

CELEBRITY INFLUENCE

Millions of teens smoke every day, even though they know it causes cancer, heart issues, and sometimes an early death. Some argue that this is partly because of the influence of celebrities. Teens see Instagram photos of Kylie Jenner with a cigarette in her mouth, and they equate these photos with what it means to be beautiful, cool, hip, and a little rebellious. As Jenna Rosenstein, a senior beauty editor for *Harper's Bazaar*, says, "a single Instagram image of a cigarette—reaching hundreds of millions of young adults—is, after all, a more effective marketing tool than anything Big Tobacco could legally publish."

This is a problem, especially when the vast amount of people who follow these celebs on Instagram are young and impressionable teens. They look to people like Jenner, Bella Hadid, Sofia Richie, and Dakota Johnson as trendsetters and often copy what they are doing.

Stephen Strasburg became an antismoking advocate after he recognized the influence that athletes can have on young fans.

(continued on the next page)

(continued from the previous page)

Aside from emulating the poses, the makeup, and the clothing, they may be imitating the smoking as well.

But some celebrities are taking a stand. Stephen Strasburg, a pitcher for the Washington Nationals, became an anti-smoking advocate after he recognized the influence that athletes and other stars have over their young fans. When he was young, he wanted to be like the major league players he saw on TV. He copied their actions. He rolled up his pants, wore wristbands, and even pinched some chewing tobacco into his lower lip. Now, years later, he is struggling with addiction and regrets the day he tried smokeless tobacco.

Strasburg has become an outspoken antismoking advocate. He discourages other high-profile baseball players from putting tins of tobacco in their back pockets or using it in front of the cameras, out of a desire to stop the next generation of teens making the same mistake he did.

less active his prefrontal cortex is. The prefrontal cortex is the part of the brain that controls decision making, learning, and other executive functions.

One of the biggest ways nicotine affects the brain is by changing the way synapses are formed. Synapses occur where nerve cells connect with other nerve cells. For example, each time a new skill is learned or a new memory is formed, stronger connections, or synapses, are created between brain cells. This process then hardwires the brain based on that experience.

Because teen brains build connections faster than adult brains, teens can become addicted much more quickly than adults. These changes make the teen brain more susceptible to drug addiction as well, meaning that teens who are addicted to nicotine are more likely to become addicted to other substances in the future. Because their brains are already hardwired to the effects of nicotine, they will respond similarly to other kinds of drugs.

WHAT IS ADDICTION?

In simple terms, being addicted means you can't give up a habit such as smoking and vaping, even though you want to. Three out of four teens who smoke in high school will still be smoking as adults, according to Smokefree.gov.

Nicotine is the chemical found in tobacco, cigarettes, and vape liquids that makes them addictive. The nicotine is absorbed quickly and goes straight to the brain. The same is true for the THC found in marijuana. Once there, these substances rewire your developing brain and train it to crave the substance. Nicotine and THC addiction can look different from person to person. Even if you only smoke or vape once in a while, you can still become addicted.

Some signs that you might be addicted to smoking or vaping include:

- Having cravings or feeling like you really need to smoke or vape

- Going to great lengths to get cigarettes, e-cigs, tobacco, or pot
- Feeling irritable, anxious, or nervous if you want to smoke or vape but can't
- Finding it hard to give up smoking or vaping even though you want to

HOW ADDICTION OCCURS

Everyone's brain is wired to make sure they repeat healthy activities such as eating a delicious meal. The brain accomplishes this task by connecting those activities with feeling good. Whenever this reward circuit is impacted, the brain makes note of the fact that something is happening that needs to be remembered. As a result, a person's brain teaches him to do that activity again and again without thinking about it.

Under normal circumstances, the reward circuit responds to feelings of pleasure by releasing dopamine.

Some signs of addiction include feeling irritable, nervous, or anxious when you want to smoke or vape but cannot.

THE COST OF SMOKING AND VAPING

Aside from the fact that smoking impacts your health, it also significantly affects your wallet. While paying a few dollars for a pack of cigarettes or an e-liquid may not seem like that big a deal, it adds up over time.

The average cost of a pack of cigarettes in the United States is $6.28, which means that if you smoke a pack of cigarettes a day, you are paying roughly $188 per month to maintain your habit. That adds up to $2,292 per year. Smoking for ten years will cost you almost $23,000. If you live in a place like New York City, where cigarettes cost $10.56 per pack on average, your out-of-pocket costs for smoking a pack a day would be $317 per month, $3,854 per year, and more than $38,000 for ten years of smoking.

But the costs of smoking do not end there. Researchers estimate that for every pack of cigarettes a person smokes, she will pay an additional $35 in health care

Smoking is an expensive habit that can cost a person nearly $4,000 a year, depending on where he lives.

(continued on the next page)

> *(continued from the previous page)*
>
> **costs. What's more, smokers usually have to pay more for life insurance, need more dental work, and have lower resale values for their homes. If you factor in the costs associated with the number of sick days a person will need to support her habit, the financial costs of smoking really start to add up. Before you know it, a lot of your hard-earned money will have gone up in smoke, along with your health.**

Dopamine is the chemical that creates those good feelings in the body. When nicotine or marijuana is inhaled through smoking or vaping, these chemicals take control of this reward system and cause large amounts of dopamine to flood the system. This flood of dopamine is what causes the excitement or happiness that is linked to smoking or vaping.

For this reason, it is easy for nicotine and marijuana to "hijack" the reward circuit and teach people to smoke or vape again and again.

But after repeated use, the brain starts to adjust to these increases in dopamine. Consequently, neurons may begin to reduce the number of dopamine receptors or simply make less dopamine. And with less dopamine signaling the brain, the ability to feel pleasure is reduced. In fact, a person may feel flat when smoking or vaping and no longer get much pleasure from it.
So, in an attempt to bring dopamine levels back up to where they were, the person may start smoking more. More nicotine or marijuana is needed to create a dopamine flood, which is an effect known as tolerance.

ADDICTION IS A DISEASE

In the past, addiction was considered a behavioral problem. In other words, people assumed that if someone truly wanted to quit smoking, she would be able to just stop. If a person had trouble quitting, she was assumed to be weak and not really motivated to quit. But researchers now know that it is not quite that simple.

As a result, the definition of addiction has changed. Now the medical community views addiction as a chronic brain disease. In other words, addiction impacts the brain's wiring and alters it permanently. Consequently, when someone is addicted to a substance like nicotine or THC, he compulsively pursues the source of his addiction, despite the fact that it harms his health. Even when someone who smokes or vapes feels like he wants to stop, he often cannot do so without help.

CHAPTER THREE

HEALTH IMPACTS OF SMOKING AND VAPING

Smoking has drastic long-term health risks. According to a 2017 report by the CDC, if teens continue to smoke at the current rates, 5.6 million of them will die early from smoking-related illnesses. That means if you take a class of twenty-six high school students, two of them will die early from smoking alone.

SMOKING: IN THE BEGINNING

When a teen first tries smoking, it is not uncommon for him to feel sick to his stomach. Some teens even throw up the first few times. After all, the body is smart and knows when it is being poisoned. Over time, the body gets used to the poison and the smoker doesn't feel sick anymore, but inside the body, the damage is still being done.

One thing that smokers may notice early on is the way that smoking impacts their lungs. Not only does smoking cause shortness of breath, coughing,

HEALTH IMPACTS OF SMOKING AND VAPING | 27

Smoking makes it hard for teens to be physically active without having trouble breathing and coughing and wheezing.

wheezing, and increased phlegm, but it also reduces lung function. As a result, when a smoker wants to do something physically active like participate in gym class, hike with friends, or go swimming, she will struggle to keep up because her lungs do not work as well as other people's.

For those who suffer from asthma, smoking can be particularly dangerous. Even if a person has not had an asthma attack for many years, taking up smoking can cause the asthma to return and make it worse over time.

HOW DO I LOOK ... AND SMELL?

Many teens start smoking because they feel it makes them look glamorous and rebellious, and they want to fit in with the popular kids. However, a 2017 study by researchers at the University of Bristol, in England, showed that people actually find smokers less attractive than their nonsmoking peers. The study was conducted using photos of identical twins, in cases where one twin smoked and the other twin didn't. Seventy percent of study participants said that the nonsmoking twin was more attractive.

Aside from the fact that smoking makes your clothing smell, it contributes to poor oral hygiene. People who smoke often have bad breath, stained or yellow teeth, and other dental hygiene issues. Smoking also causes early skin damage and lots of wrinkles. In fact, people who smoke often have skin that looks leathery and dull.

HOW SMOKING AFFECTS YOUR BODY

Once you get used to smoking you may feel like it's not having much of an impact on your body. The truth is that every cigarette you smoke is doing damage, not only to your lungs but also to your brain, heart, mouth, throat, and skin.

SMOKING AFFECTS YOUR BRAIN

If you smoke, you are more likely to have a stroke than someone who does not smoke. In fact, smoking increases the risk that you will have a stroke by at least 50 percent, according to the National Health Service (NHS), the public health agency in the United Kingdom, and your chances of dying from a stroke are doubled. The good news is that within two years of stopping smoking, your risk of stroke is reduced by half, and within five years it will be the same as a nonsmoker's.

SMOKING AFFECTS YOUR HEART

Smoking damages your heart and increases your risk of heart disease, heart attack, and stroke. It also damages your blood vessels and your arteries, even the ones that supply blood to your brain. In fact, smoking doubles your risk of having a heart attack and dying from heart disease, according to the NHS. On the other hand, one year after quitting smoking your risk is reduced by half, and fifteen years after quitting your risk is similar to that of someone who has never smoked.

SMOKING AFFECTS YOUR LUNGS

Aside from the fact that smoking makes you cough, catch colds, wheeze, and have asthma flares, it is

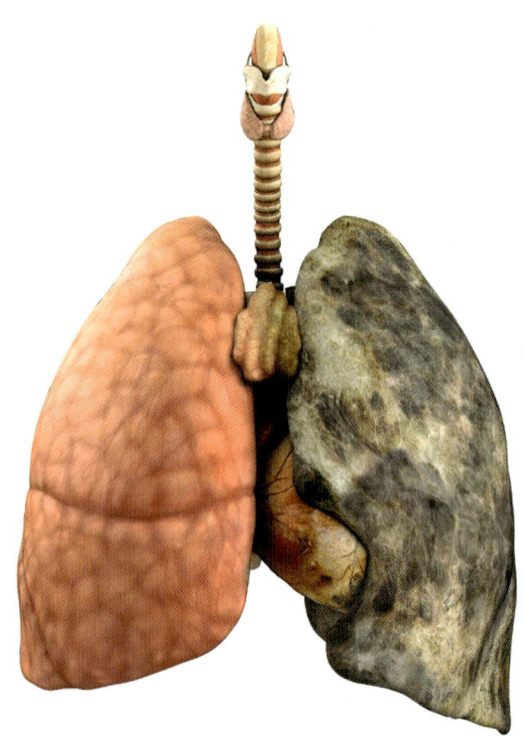

extremely damaging to your lungs. Smoking causes many fatal diseases like pneumonia, emphysema, and lung cancer. What's more, smoking causes 84 percent of all lung cancer deaths and 83 percent of deaths from chronic obstructive pulmonary disease (COPD), according to the NHS.

SMOKING AFFECTS YOUR MOUTH AND THROAT

Smoking causes 84 percent of all lung cancer deaths and 83 percent of deaths from COPD, according to the National Health Service.

In addition to bad breath and yellow teeth, smoking can cause gum disease and damage your sense of taste. You are also at risk for cancer of the tongue, lips, throat, and voice box. In fact, more than 93 percent of cancers in the throat are caused by smoking. But if you quit smoking, your risk of these cancers goes down. In fact, after twenty years of being smoke-free, your risk of cancers in these areas is reduced to that of a nonsmoker.

SMOKING AFFECTS YOUR SKIN

Smoking can make your skin age more quickly as well as look gray and dull. This happens because

CYCLIC VOMITING SYNDROME AND CANNABINOID HYPEREMESIS SYNDROME

Although marijuana use doesn't come with the same risks as smoking cigarettes, heavy marijuana use has been linked with two conditions known as cyclic vomiting syndrome (CVS) and cannabinoid hyperemesis syndrome (CHS). Both syndromes cause extreme nausea, vomiting, and severe abdominal pain for hours, or even days, at a time.

Robert Glatter, a doctor at Lenox Hill Hospital, says it took a long time for the medical community to recognize that marijuana was linked to CVS because marijuana is typically thought to reduce nausea. "I would see people in the emergency department with heavy and chronic [marijuana] use who would have these vomiting syndromes with abdominal pain, and we just didn't know what it was."

Some researchers consider CHS a subset of CVS, and a study in *German Medical Science* suggests that the only way to distinguish the two conditions is that the symptoms of CHS go away completely after the person stops using marijuana.

the amount of oxygen that gets to your skin is drastically reduced. In fact, smoking can age your skin prematurely by as much as twenty years, according to the NHS. You are also more likely to develop wrinkles, especially around the eyes and mouth.

SMOKING AFFECTS YOUR ENTIRE BODY

There is not a single area of your body that is not impacted by smoking. For instance, smoking can make your bones weak and brittle. It also can lead to stomach ulcers, bladder cancer, kidney cancer, and cervical cancer. In addition, smoking can lower your sperm count and make it more difficult for you to have children. According to the NHS, the fertility of women who smoke is only 72 percent of that of nonsmoking women.

IS VAPING THE LESSER OF TWO EVILS?

Many people choose to vape instead of smoking because they believe it is a healthier option. But vaping comes with many serious health risks. Until 2016, the Food and Drug Administration (FDA) had no oversight of e-cigarettes. Now, thanks to the Family Smoking Prevention and Tobacco Control Act, the FDA monitors the safety of all tobacco products, including e-cigarettes and hookah tobacco, with the goal of increasing awareness of the health risks of e-cigarettes and other tobacco products.

HEALTH IMPACTS OF SMOKING AND VAPING | 33

E-cigarettes contain chemicals that are known to cause cancer, such as formaldehyde and acetaldehyde.

Early studies show that most e-cigarettes and e-liquids contain a number of harmful ingredients. Although e-cigarettes don't produce tobacco smoke, they still contain nicotine, which is damaging to brain development and therefore particularly harmful for teenagers. The nicotine means that vaping is just as addictive as smoking cigarettes, and in fact, teens who vape are more likely to move on to smoking traditional cigarettes as well. Moreover, some e-cigarettes contain chemicals that are known to cause cancer, such as formaldehyde and acetaldehyde, as well as possibly toxic metal nanoparticles from the vaporizer itself.

In January 2018, an FDA panel voted in support of a claim by cigarette company Phillip Morris that its iQOS vaping system reduces exposure to harmful chemicals because it heats tobacco but doesn't ignite it. However, the panel did not endorse the company's claim that this system reduces the user's risk for tobacco-related diseases.

WHAT DOES VAPING HAVE TO DO WITH "POPCORN LUNG"?

Diacetyl is a buttery-flavored chemical sometimes found in popcorn, caramel, potato chips, crackers, corn chips, and many dairy products. In 2007, the country's major popcorn manufacturers began removing it from their products after they discovered the workers in the factory were getting sick from breathing it in. In fact, diacetyl has been linked to hundreds of cases of bronchiolitis obliterans, a serious and irreversible lung disease. This disease is sometimes called popcorn lung.

When diacetyl is inhaled, it can scar the tiny air sacs in the lungs. This, in turn, results in the thickening and narrowing of airways. People with popcorn lung often cough, wheeze, and experience shortness of breath. These symptoms are similar to the symptoms people with COPD (chronic obstructive pulmonary disease) experience.

Despite the known risks of diacetyl, this chemical is often added to e-cigarette liquids to complement the other flavorings. As a result, many people who vape are inhaling this harmful chemical into their lungs and are at risk of developing popcorn lung.

Researchers at Harvard T. H. Chan Schools of Public Health found that thirty-nine out of fifty-one e-cigarette brands contained diacetyl, according to a 2015 report. The study also found that many e-cigarettes contained the chemicals pentanedione and acetoin, which cause respiratory problems. Roughly 92 percent of all e-cigarettes tested had one of the three chemicals in its blends.

CHAPTER FOUR

BE A QUITTER!

Once addicted, most smokers will tell you that they spend a large amount of time thinking about how they wished they didn't smoke. But nicotine and marijuana are powerful substances, and once people are addicted, they feel like they cannot function without them. They look forward to the next time they can do it and get annoyed when they cannot. That is what addiction feels like.

By the time most people reach this point, they have realized that quitting is going to be harder than they thought. Most experts say it usually takes around ten tries before someone who smokes or vapes manages to quit for good.

REASONS WHY YOU SHOULD QUIT NOW

One of the best gifts you can give yourself is to quit smoking and vaping. Not only does smoking and vaping harm your health, but it also impacts the health of

BE A QUITTER! | 37

Experts say it usually takes around ten tries before someone who smokes or vapes manages to quit for good.

those around you. Plus, when you quit smoking or vaping, your body will start to feel better. In fact, according to the surgeon general, smokers who quit before the age of thirty will undo much of the health-related damage done by smoking. According to the American Cancer Society, there are a number of other reasons why it's a good idea to quit smoking while you are young.

It reduces your risk of heart issues. In fact, just one year after quitting smoking, the risk of a heart attack drops significantly.

It reduces your risk of stroke. Within two to five years after you quit smoking, your risk of a stroke may be equal to that of a nonsmoker's risk.

It reduces your risk of certain cancers. After you quit smoking, your risk of cancers of the mouth, esophagus, throat, and bladder drop by half within five years.

It reduces your risk of lung cancer. Once you have been smoke-free for ten years, your risk of developing lung cancer drops by half.

Whatever your personal reasons are for quitting, take a minute to write them down. Then, post them somewhere where you will see them every time you reach for a cigarette, a joint, or your vape pen.

PREPARING TO QUIT

Once you have made the decision to quit smoking or vaping, you need to be sure you are prepared for all that it entails. For instance, most teens who smoke or vape have friends who also smoke or vape. If you want to quit and your friends do not, it could change some of your relationships.

Overall, your friendships should make you feel good about who you are. If your friends are not supportive of your desire to quit smoking or vaping, or if they pressure you not to quit, then it may be time to start hanging out with different people. The important thing to remember is that smoking and vaping do

Most teens who smoke or vape have friends who also smoke or vape. If you want to quit and your friends do not, your relationships could become strained.

not define you. True friends enjoy spending time with you because of who you are, not because you smoke or vape with them.

You also may want to avoid events and activities where you know that people will be smoking and vaping. Putting yourself in those situations only makes it harder for you to be successful. It might help to explain to your friends that you are not trying to avoid them; you just need to avoid any situation where you might be tempted to smoke or vape.

STRATEGIES FOR QUITTING SMOKING AND VAPING

Quitting smoking or vaping is not an easy task, but there are a number of different tools out there to help you quit. From patches and gum to lozenges and apps, you have a lot to choose from. The key is to come up with a plan that will work for you. There are a number of things you should consider as you prepare to quit.

THINK ABOUT WHY YOU ARE QUITTING

Begin by making a list of why you want to quit and what you hope to change about your life. It also helps to write down any goals you hope to accomplish along the way. Knowing why you are quitting and how you want your life to change will keep you motivated when things get tough.

TALK TO A DOCTOR

If you think you might like to try a cessation aid like a nicotine patch or gum, talk to your doctor. There are some cessation aids that can be bought over the counter, but there are others that require a prescription. Your doctor can tell you what is safe and how to use these aids effectively.

BE A QUITTER! | 41

Some cessation aids can be bought over the counter, but there are others that require a prescription. Talk to your doctor before trying a cessation aid like a nicotine patch or gum.

COME UP WITH A PLAN

Take some time to think about how you are going to fight cravings and deal with withdrawal. You also can try some of the free tools out there like the SmokeFreeTXT, which is a texting program designed for thirteen- to nineteen-year-olds. For six to eight weeks, you will receive three to five texts a day with tips, advice, and encouragement. Another option is the quitSTART app. This free smartphone app takes the information you provide about your smoking or vaping habits and gives you tips, inspiration, and challenges to help you quit smoking or vaping and live a healthier life.

AVOID TEMPTATIONS

Think about what makes you want to smoke or vape. If there are certain people, places, or things that make you want to smoke or vape, plan on how you can avoid these situations. Knowing ahead of time how to avoid your triggers will make quitting so much easier.

REWARD YOURSELF

Set small goals for yourself and then be sure to reward yourself when you are successful. One option is to set aside the money you normally spend on smoking or vaping. Then, when you reach a milestone, buy yourself something nice, take a friend to dinner, or make a donation to a charity. The key is to celebrate your successes.

KEEP A POSITIVE OUTLOOK

It is not easy to quit smoking or vaping. In fact, there are days when it will be downright difficult. As a result, it is very important that you try to stay positive and remind yourself why you are quitting. It also can help to distract yourself by doing something fun.

DON'T GIVE IN TO YOUR CRAVINGS, EVEN ONCE

When you quit, you will probably have strong urges to smoke or vape. It may feel like they will never go away. But the cravings will go away after time, as long as you don't give in to them. Every time you do lapse and have "just one" cigarette or e-cigarette, you are essentially going back to square one, because your cravings will get worse again. But if you stay strong and don't give in to your cravings, they will go away eventually.

ASK FOR HELP

Remember, you do not have to do this alone. In fact, it helps to have a support system when you quit smoking and vaping. Not only can friends encourage you, but they also can hold you accountable. Many other people have quit smoking or vaping and they can offer ideas on how to kick the habit.

There are also resources available to help you stay on track if you are struggling. There is even a toll-free number (1-800-QUIT-NOW) that you call can anytime to get help and support. Advocates that work for these service providers understand what you are going

When you are trying to quit smoking, it can help to distract yourself by doing something fun or spending time with friends who support your decision.

through. They can help you get back on track and remember why you wanted to quit in the first place.

"[Remember,] the best part about quitting is that you are creating a new life for yourself," says Joe, a former smoker who shared his story with Verywell.com. "We become completely different people when we quit smoking."

CHAPTER FIVE

CHOOSING TO BE SMOKE FREE

Being a teenager can be downright stressful. You may feel stressed if your parents put pressure on you to do well in school or sports. You may feel stressed when you are in a hurry, you have too many things to do, or you have a lot of homework. Even trying to fit in at school can make you feel stressed. You might worry about what to say, what to wear, and how you look.

Stress is caused by your emotions, but it also affects your mood and your body. You probably know what stress feels like in your own body. It may cause you to feel a tightness in your shoulders and neck, or you might feel sick to your stomach. It may even make your heart beat faster and give you a headache.

When you are feeling stressed, it is normal to want to feel better. Many teens turn to cigarettes or vaping to relieve the stress. But reaching for a cigarette, a joint, or a vape pen is not a long-term solution. In fact, this is what experts call a negative coping strategy. Negative coping strategies don't fix the problem, and they actually make the situation worse in the long term.

When you are feeling stressed, it is normal to want to feel better. But reaching for a cigarette or a vape pen is not a long-term solution.

Once your body becomes addicted to these habits and substances, your stress will increase. Not only will your original problems still be there when you are done smoking and vaping, but now you have the added stress of addiction. As you become more addicted, your cravings for nicotine will cause you to feel even more stressed.

Fortunately, there are a number of healthy strategies you can use to relieve your stress.

TIPS FOR DESTRESSING YOUR LIFE

Healthy coping strategies are safe, effective ways to deal with your problems without damaging your health and making the problem worse.

GET MOVING

One of the best ways to bust the stress in your life is through physical activity. That doesn't mean you have to join a running club if you hate running, nor does it mean that you have to do yoga or dance if that is not your thing. The key is to discover what type of physical activity you do enjoy. From skateboarding and canoeing to hiking and cycling, there are lots of options out there. The most important thing is to keep moving.

Physical activity is one of the best ways to relieve stress. Think about what type of physical activity you enjoy and go from there.

SCHEDULE TIME FOR FUN

While it is true that school, sports, band practice, and other extracurricular activities are important, they should not take up all your time. Make sure to schedule time for fun activities too. Then, when it's time for your fun activity, tell yourself you are not going to think about school, homework, or sports.

GET SOME SLEEP

According to the American Psychological Association's Stress in America survey, teens need nine hours of sleep a night, but most of them are getting less than seven and a half hours a night. When you are getting enough sleep, your stress levels—and your mood—will improve dramatically.

BE PRACTICAL, NOT PERFECT

If you feel overwhelmed by the number of things you have to do, learn how to break them into smaller, more manageable tasks. If your parents stress you out with their expectations, talk to them about how you feel. Also, don't try to be perfect. Instead, be content with doing your best. Remember, perfection is unattainable and trying to achieve it will only make you more stressed out.

TALK ABOUT IT

Managing the stress in your life is so much easier when you have a support system. Talking about your feelings instead of keeping them bottled up inside or trying to handle them alone will do wonders for your stress levels. Your friends and family might be able to offer some ideas on how to handle the pressures you are feeling. If your family isn't helping, seek out another adult you can discuss this with, such as a teacher or guidance counselor.

TRYING TO FIT IN—THE STRUGGLE IS REAL

Just about every teen wants to fit in at school. Figuring out who you are and where you belong is not an easy task, and if you feel that you don't fit in at all, it can be pretty lonely. Wanting to be popular is completely normal, but choosing to smoke or vape is not the way to go about achieving it. Chasing after popularity is not only exhausting and stressful, but it doesn't allow you to be who you truly are. It may seem hard right now, but if you embrace who you are, instead of trying to be like everyone else, you will likely find more genuine friendships in the long term. Remember, your little quirks and differences are what make you interesting. Be proud of them.

STANDING UP TO PEER PRESSURE

Adults talk a lot about saying no to smoking and vaping. While many of their suggestions are useful, sometimes saying no is not as easy as it sounds. Peer pressure is real, but you can stand up to it if you are prepared.

FIND YOUR STRENGTH IN NUMBERS

While it may seem like everyone's smoking or vaping, there are bound to be other teens like you who don't

Being prepared is one of the best ways to deal with peer pressure. Practice what you are going to do or say and make sure you have a few friends who have your back.

want to do it. Talk to your friends who do not smoke or vape about how you are feeling. Chances are, they are feeling the same way. And, if you band together and have each other's back, you are less likely to give in when others pressure you to smoke.

BE AWARE OF YOUR MOODS

If you go to a party in a bad mood or while you are angry with your parents, you may be more likely to do something rebellious like smoking. If you notice that you are not feeling like yourself, whether you're angry, sad, or anxious, try to avoid situations where you might be tempted to compromise your values.

USE A WITTY COMEBACK

Sometimes humor helps to diffuse an awkward situation. If someone urges you to smoke pot, you could say something like, "I like my brain the way it is, thank you very much." Or, if someone offers you a drag off his or her cigarette, you could laugh and say, "I don't want to have ashtray breath if I meet the man of my dreams tonight."

BE CONFIDENT IN YOUR DECISION

If someone offers you a cigarette, make eye contact and say, "No, thank you" in a confident voice. The more certain you are when you refuse to smoke or vape, the less others will bug you about it. Also, remember that "no" is enough. You do not owe anyone an explanation for why you don't want to smoke or vape.

BE A LEADER

Often the leaders in school are the ones who are not afraid to be assertive or express their opinions. Everyone can be a leader if they are confident in their decisions. When you choose to be smoke free, you have an opportunity to be a positive role model for your peers and help others stay smoke free too.

When you see someone else take a stand against smoking and vaping, be sure you support her. It is hard to say no when you have the impression that everyone else in your group is doing it. But if you lend your support, there is strength in numbers. What's more, your support might just give someone else the courage to stay smoke free!

10 GREAT QUESTIONS TO ASK A DOCTOR

1. How can I tell if I am addicted to smoking or vaping?
2. How can I quit smoking or vaping?
3. Do nicotine patches and gum work? What are the best and safest cessation aids?
4. If I can't quit nicotine, should I start vaping instead of smoking?
5. What is the least dangerous vaping product or device to use?
6. Where can I get more support to help me stop smoking or vaping?
7. What sort of withdrawal symptoms will I experience?
8. How can I deal with cravings when I am trying to quit?
9. How can I deal with stress if I can't smoke or vape?
10. When will I stop having cravings to smoke and vape?

GLOSSARY

addiction Persistent, compulsive use of a substance.

asthma A respiratory condition that causes wheezing, coughing, and difficulty breathing when the bronchial tubes become irritated.

bidis A thin, hand-rolled cigarette made with tobacco, often wrapped in leaves.

COPD Chronic obstructive pulmonary disease. A chronic lung disease that is characterized by obstructed airflow to the lungs.

diacetyl A chemical that damages the air sacs in the lungs when inhaled.

dopamine A chemical messenger released in the body that causes "feel good" sensations.

e-cigarettes A battery-operated device that simulates smoking by vaporizing a liquid that the user inhales.

heart attack Sudden and sometimes fatal damage to part of the heart muscle.

heart disease A range of conditions that damage the heart; also known as cardiovascular disease.

hookah An instrument for vaporizing and smoking tobacco; the tobacco is drawn through a water basin and inhaled.

Juul A brand of vape pen that is particularly small and discreet.

marijuana A drug made from the cannabis plant that can be smoked or eaten; in some states it is legal for people over the age of twenty-one.

nicotine A toxic chemical found in tobacco that acts as a stimulant when smoked or used in smokeless forms and causes addiction.

phlegm A thick substance secreted by the mucous membranes in the lungs.

popcorn lung Also known as bronchiolitis obliterans; a lung disease caused by inhaling the chemical diacetyl.

prefrontal cortex The part of the brain responsible for making decisions, personality expression, and moderating social behavior.

smokeless tobacco Tobacco that is chewed or sniffed rather than smoked.

stroke A medical emergency that occurs when blood flow to the brain is cut off.

synapses The gap between nerve cells where impulses pass through.

THC Tetrahydrocannabinol; the primary active ingredient in marijuana.

tobacco A product made from tobacco leaves that are dried for the purpose of smoking or chewing.

vape pen An electronic pen- or cigar-shaped device that heats and vaporizes liquid, usually containing nicotine and other chemicals, for the user to inhale.

vaping The act of inhaling the vapor produced by an e-cigarette or a vape pen.

FOR MORE INFORMATION

American Lung Association
55 W. Wacker Drive, Suite 1150
Chicago, IL 60601
(1-800) LUNGUSA
Website: http://www.lung.org/stop-smoking
Facebook: @lungusa
Twitter: @LungAssociation
This is a nonprofit organization that works to improve lung health through research, education, and advocacy. The website contains information on smoking, how it harms your body, and how you can quit.

American Society of Addiction Medicine
11400 Rockville Pike, Suite 200
Rockville, MD 20852
(301) 656-3920
Website: https://www.asam.org
Facebook: @addictionmedicine
Instagram and Twitter: @ASAMorg
This professional medical society is dedicated to improving addiction treatment, supporting research, and educating professionals and the public about addiction. The website offers a directory of addiction medicine professionals.

Canadian Cancer Society: Smoker's Helpline
(1-800) 513-5333
Facebook and Twitter: @SmokersHelpline

FOR MORE INFORMATION

Website: https://www.smokershelpline.ca
This national organization of volunteers is committed to eradicating cancer and improving the quality of life of people living with cancer. The Support and Services section offers a helpline for those trying to quit smoking, as well as comprehensive resources.

Centers for Disease Control and Prevention: Youth Tobacco Prevention
1600 Clifton Road
Atlanta, GA 30329
(800) CDC-INFO (800-232-4636)
(1-800) QUIT-NOW
Website: https://www.cdc.gov/tobacco/basic_information/youth
Facebook and Twitter: @CDCTobaccoFree
The leading federal agency for tobacco prevention and control, this organization provides information, tips, and a hotline for young people trying to quit smoking.

Health Canada: Smoking and Tobacco
Address Locator 0900C2
Ottawa, ON K1A 0K9
Canada
(613) 957-2991
Website: https://www.canada.ca/en/health-canada/services/smoking-tobacco.html
The Canadian government's website provides comprehensive information on tobacco use data, the effects of smoking, prevention, and how to quit.

National Center on Addiction and Substance Abuse
633 Third Avenue
New York, NY 10017
(212) 841-5200
Website: https://www.centeronaddiction.org
Facebook: @CenterOnAddiction
Twitter: @CASAaddiction
This research and policy organization focuses on improving the understanding of addiction, as well as treatment and prevention.

Smokefree Teen
US Department of Health and Human Services
200 Independence Avenue SW
Washington, DC 20201
(877) 696-6775
Website: https://teen.smokefree.gov
This website provides a variety of information and resources for teens, with apps and texting programs to help teens quit smoking.

Smoking Stinks
Anne Arundel County Department of Health
3 Harry S. Truman Parkway
Annapolis, MD
(410) 222-7979
Website: https://teens.smokingstinks.org
This website offers resources for teens and kids with tips on how to stay smoke free as well as downloads, e-cards, and games.

FOR FURTHER READING

Carr, Allan. *Your Personal Stop Smoking Plan*. London, UK: Arcturus Publishing, 2015.

Chase, Reeve, and Frederick Gross. *The Truth About Marijuana*. New York, NY: Rosen Publishing, 2012.

Espejo, Roman. *Teen Smoking* (Teen Issues). New York, NY: Greenhaven Publishing, 2015.

Espejo, Roman. *Tobacco and Smoking* (Opposing Viewpoints). New York, NY: Greenhaven Publishing, 2015.

Espejo, Roman. *Tobacco and Smoking* (Teen Rights and Freedoms). New York, NY: Greenhaven Publishing, 2014.

Hollander, Barbara. *Addiction: Understanding Brain Diseases and Disorders*. New York, NY: Rosen Publishing, 2012.

Keyishian, Elizabeth, and Veronica Stollers. *Frequently Asked Questions About Smoking*. New York, NY: Rosen Publishing, 2012.

Marijuana: Abuse and Legalization. New York, NY: Greenhaven Publishing, 2016.

Rebman, Renee C. *Are You Doing Risky Things?* New York, NY: Enslow Publishers, 2015.

Scott, Victor. *Vaping: The Hazardous Effects of Looking Cool*. Amazon Digital Services LLC, 2017.

BIBLIOGRAPHY

American Cancer Society. "Benefits of Quitting Smoking Over Time." Stay Away from Tobacco, September 9, 2016. https://www.cancer.org/healthy/stay-away-from-tobacco/benefits-of-quitting-smoking-over-time.html.

American Lung Association. "Popcorn Lung: A Dangerous Risk of Flavored E-Cigarettes." July 7, 2016. http://www.lung.org/about-us/blog/2016/07/popcorn-lung-risk-ecigs.html.

American Lung Association. "Why Kids Start Smoking." Smoking Facts. Retrieved January 31, 2018. http://www.lung.org/stop-smoking/smoking-facts/why-kids-start-smoking.html.

Blumentrath, Christian G., Boris Dohrmann, and Nils Ewald. "Cannabinoid Hyperemesis and the Cyclic Vomiting Syndrome in Adults: Recognition, Diagnosis, Acute and Long-Term Treatment." GMS German Medical Science, March 21, 2017. https://www.ncbi.nlm.nih.gov/pmc/articles/PMC5360975/.

Centers for Disease Control and Prevention. "Youth and Tobacco Use." Smoking and Tobacco Use, September 20, 2017. https://www.cdc.gov/tobacco/data_statistics/fact_sheets/youth_data/tobacco_use/index.htm.

Grillo, Jerry. "Teen Vaping: What You Should Know." WebMD, August 3, 2016. https://www.webmd.com/smoking-cessation/features/teen-vaping#1.

Linton, Alaya. "How Much Money Does Smoking Cost You?" Balance, June 27, 2017. https://thebalance.com/how-much-money-does-smoking-cost-you-4143324.

National Health Service. "How Smoking Affects Your Body." Smokefree. Retrieved January 31, 2018. https://www.nhs.uk/smokefree/why-quit/smoking-health-problems.

National Institutes of Health. "Encoded Exposure to Tobacco Use in Social Media Predicts Subsequent Smoking Behavior." U.S. National Library of Medicine, March 2015.

Raloff, Janet. "Teen Vaping Soars Past Cigarette Use." Science News for Students, April 28, 2016. https://www.sciencenewsforstudents.org/article/teen-vaping-soars-past-cigarette-use.

Rosenstein, Jenna. "Why Is Everyone Smoking Again?" *Harper's Bazaar*, May 16, 2017. http://www.harpersbazaar.com/beauty/a9554018/smoking-on-instagram.

Stein, Rob. "FDA Panel Gives Qualified Support to Claims for 'Safer' Smoking Device." NPR, January 25, 2018. https://www.npr.org.

US Department of Health and Human Services. "E-Cigarette Use Among Youth and Young Adults." A Report from the Surgeon General. Retrieved December 31, 2017. https://e-cigarettes.surgeongeneral.gov/documents/2016_SGR_Fact_Sheet_508.pdf.

US Department of Health and Human Services. "Know the Risks: E-Cigarettes & Young People." Surgeon General. Retrieved December 31, 2017. https://e-cigarettes.surgeongeneral.gov/getthefacts.html.

Wheeler, Mark. "Tobacco Impacts Teens' Brains, UCLA Study Shows." UCLA Newsroom, March 2, 2011. http://newsroom.ucla.edu/releases/teen-brains-impacted-by-smoking-192660.

INDEX

A

addiction
  occurrence of, 22, 24
  seeking help with, 43, 44
  and teens, 20, 21
  what is, 21
American Lung Association, 13
asthma, 4, 27, 29

B

bidis, 9, 12–13
Big Tobacco, 19
Buerger's disease, 7

C

cannabinoid hyperemesis syndrome (CHS), 31
cessation aids, 40
Centers for Disease Control and Prevention (CDC), 5, 6, 7, 16, 26
chronic obstructive pulmonary disease (COPD), 34
cigarettes, 5
  addiction to, 16, 17, 20, 21
  cravings, 21, 41
  ingredients in, 9, 10
  overcoming, 43
  popularity of, 6, 7, 8
  and stress, 46
cyclic vomiting syndrome (CVS), 31

D

destressing, 47, 48
diacetyl, 34, 35
dopamine, 22–23, 24

E

e-cigarettes, 10, 11, 16
  contents of, 7–8, 33, 35
  popularity of, 6, 8, 17
emphysema, 30

F

Family Smoking Prevention and Tobacco Control Act, 32
Food and Drug Administration (FDA), 28, 32

H

heart attack, 29, 37
heart disease, 7, 10, 12, 29
hookah, 9, 12, 32

I

Instagram, 19

INDEX

J
Jenner, Kylie, 19
Juul, 9

L
lung cancer, 4, 5, 7, 30, 38
lung disease, 10, 11, 12, 30, 34

M
marijuana, 9, 11–12, 21, 24, 31, 36

N
National Health Service (NHS), 29
nicotine, 13, 16, 18, 20, 21, 24, 25
   addiction to, 36, 40
   cravings, 46
   and vaping, 33

P
peer pressure, 14
   standing up to, 50
Phillip Morris, 34
popcorn lung, 34, 35

S
smokeless tobacco, 9, 11, 20
smoker, becoming a, 13, 14

smoking
   advertisement of, 14
   cost of, 23, 24
   early health impacts of, 28
   effect on attractiveness, 28
   effect on brain, 29
   effect on heart, 29
   effect on lungs, 29–30
   effect on mouth and throat, 30
   effect on skin, 31, 32
   effect on whole body, 32
   quitting, 36, 37, 38, 39
   and teenagers, 13, 14
Strasburg, Stephen, 19, 20
stress, 45
   overcoming, 47, 48, 49
   and smoking, 45, 46
synapses, 20

T
THC, 21, 25

V
vape pen, 10, 38, 45
vaping
   addiction to, 21, 22, 24, 46
   health risks of, 7, 17, 33, 34
   vs. smoking, 6, 32, 33

ABOUT THE AUTHOR

Sherri Mabry Gordon is a bullying prevention advocate and author of numerous nonfiction books. Many of her books deal with issues teens face today, including bullying, abuse, public shaming, online safety, and more. Gordon also writes about bullying, dating violence, and other teen issues for Verywell.com. She has given multiple presentations at schools, churches, and the YMCA on bullying prevention, dating abuse, and online safety, and she volunteers regularly. She also serves on the school counselor advisory board for two schools. Gordon resides in Columbus, Ohio, with her husband, two children, and dog, Abbey.

PHOTO CREDITS

Cover Diego Cervo/Shutterstock.com; back cover Photo by Marianna armata/Moment/Getty Images; p. 5 ucchie79/shutterstock.com; pp. 7, 16, 26, 36, 45 (background) Hazem.m.kamal/Shutterstock.com; p. 8 Jeff Greenberg/Photolibrary/Getty Images; p. 10 Charlotte Observer/Tribune News Service/Getty Images; p. 13 Fly Fernandez/Corbis/Getty Images; p. 14 Alessio Botticelli/GC Images/Getty Images; p. 17 Ramin Talaie/Corbis Historical/Getty Images; p. 18 Studio ART/Shutterstock.com; p. 19 Paul Bereswill/Getty Images; p. 22 BCFC/Shutterstock.com; p. 23 Smith Collection/The Image Bank/Getty Images; p. 27 Chris Cole/The Image Bank/Getty Images; p. 30 Linda Bucklin/Shutterstock.com; p. 33 NeydtStock/Shutterstock.com; p. 37 Sangaroon/Shutterstock.com; p. 39 JGI/Jamie Grill/Blend Images/Getty Images; p. 41 Jeff Greenberg/Universal Images Group/Getty Images; p. 44 Solis Images/Shutterstock.com; p. 46 Iam_Anupong/Shutterstock.com; p. 47 goodluz/Shutterstock.com; p. 50 Monkey Business Images/Shutterstock.com.

Design: Michael Moy; Layout and Photo Research: Ellina Litmanovich; Editor: Rachel Aimee